A Note to Parents and Caregivers:

Read-it! Readers are for children who are just starting on the amazing road to reading. These beautiful books support both the acquisition of reading skills and the love of books.

The PURPLE LEVEL presents basic topics and objects using high frequency words and simple language patterns.

The RED LEVEL presents familiar topics using common words and repeating sentence patterns.

The BLUE LEVEL presents new ideas using a larger vocabulary and varied sentence structure.

The YELLOW LEVEL presents more challenging ideas, a broad vocabulary, and wide variety in sentence structure.

The GREEN LEVEL presents more complex ideas, an extended vocabulary range, and expanded language structures.

The ORANGE LEVEL presents a wide range of ideas and concepts using challenging vocabulary and complex language structures.

When sharing a book with your child, read in short stretches, pausing often to talk about the pictures. Have your child turn the pages and point to the pictures and familiar words. And be sure to reread favorite stories or parts of stories.

There is no right or wrong way to share books with children. Find time to read with your child, and pass on the legacy of literacy.

Adria F. Klein, Ph.D.
Professor Emeritus
California State University
San Bernardino, California

First American edition published in 2005 by
Picture Window Books
5115 Excelsior Boulevard
Suite 232
Minneapolis, MN 55416
877-845-8392
www.picturewindowbooks.com

First published in Canada in 1999 by
Les éditions Héritage inc.
300 Arran Street, Saint Lambert
Quebec, Canada J4R 1K5

Printed in the United States of America.

Library of Congress Cataloging-in-Publication Data
Villeneuve, Mireille.
A clown in love / written by Mireille Villeneuve ; illustrated by Anne Villeneuve.
p. cm. — (Read it! readers)
Summary: Felicio tries to help his father, a clown, win the love of Sophie the acrobat.
ISBN 1-4048-1069-2 (hardcover)
[1. Circus—Fiction. 2. Love—Fiction.] I. Villeneuve, Anne, ill. II. Title. III. Series.

PZ7.V73Cl 2004
[E]—dc22
                                                                    2004025403

A Clown in Love

By Mireille Villeneuve
Illustrated by Anne Villeneuve

Special thanks to our advisers for their expertise:

Adria F. Klein, Ph.D.
Professor Emeritus, California State University
San Bernardino, California

Susan Kesselring, M.A.
Literacy Educator
Rosemount - Apple Valley - Eagan (Minnesota) School District

PICTURE WINDOW BOOKS
Minneapolis, Minnesota

Felicio is worried. His father has a strange disease.

But this isn't the first time that Mr. Bartholemy has caught this virus. The last time, he was sick for a long time.

Mr. Bartholemy does incredible things when he has this virus.

In the morning, he smiles at his bowl of cereal. Other times, in the middle of a conversation, he looks at his feet and sighs.

This time, Mr. Bartholemy seems really sick with the disease. He has never acted so strange. Before going to work, he picks a whole bunch of flowers saying a little rhyme, "She loves me, she loves me not, she loves me, she loves me not."

Then he knocks at the window of his neighbor. Beautiful Sophie receives a huge bouquet of flowers—that sprays her from head to toe.

Yes, Felicio is certain his father has "caught" love. For a clown, it is a terrible disease. Who will take him seriously?

Felicio looks quickly for a cure.
He finds it in the fairy tale
Cinderella. The boy sneaks
away with a shoe from
Sophie's house. It's a
tiny shoe.

"Look, Dad, surely it belongs to
beautiful Sophie!" says Felicio.

Right away, his father runs, jumps, and takes off to see Sophie.

"Oh, thank you, Mr. Bartholemy. You have found the little shoe of my chimpanzee, Lily!" Sophie says.

Sophie gives a sweet, gentle kiss—to her chimpanzee!

"I guess she only likes furry animals with big smiles," the sad clown says to himself.

Felicio thinks about his favorite fairy tale, *Beauty and the Beast*. He finds a costume of a huge, scary beast for his father.

With his furry body and his big, clawed feet, Mr. Bartholemy should be irresistible. Lily is charmed, but Sophie escapes by running away!

19

Felicio must find a more romantic story—like *Romeo and Juliet*. Mr. Bartholemy climbs up to Sophie's window. He whispers pretty poems into her hairy ear.

Hairy? Poor Mr. Bartholemy! Lily doesn't like poetry.

In order to make his father feel better, Felicio tells him the story of *Sleeping Beauty*. In the middle of his story, Felicio suddenly stops.

That's it! He's found it! Sophie will be Sleeping Beauty and his father can wake her with a sweet kiss.

First, he must make Sophie fall asleep. He makes a huge pot of calming tea. But Mr. Bartholemy knows a better potion for lovebirds. Secretly, he makes a passion fruit tea.

That night, Felicio and Lily and the two lovebirds have tea. Mr. Bartholemy serves everyone. In Sophie's cup and in his own, he puts the passion fruit tea. Then in Felicio's cup and in Lily's, he puts the calming tea.

All evening long, Sophie and the clown look at each other lovingly. Next to them, Felicio and Lily dream wonderful dreams.

The next day, Mr. Bartholemy really has his head in the clouds. During the show, his big clown get caught up in the tight rope. It's a catastrophe! Felicio doesn't dare look.

When Felicio opens his eyes, he is very
surprised. Sophie dives and falls—right into
his father's arms.

The beautiful tightrope walker is very moved.
She stumbles over her words. "You are the best
clown—I mean acrobat—that I know. Would
you like to be my partner, um, and also my
boyfriend?"

"Yes, I would," responds Mr. Bartholemy with
his sweetest clown smile.

At the same time, Felicio runs and catches ...

Lily the chimpanzee who gives him a big, wet kiss!

More *Read-it!* Readers

Bright pictures and fun stories help you practice your reading skills. Look for more books at your level.

A Clown in Love by Mireille Villeneuve
Alex and the Game of the Century by Gilles Tibo
Alex and Toolie by Gilles Tibo
Daddy's an Alien by Bruno St-Aubin
Emily Lee Carole Temblay
Forrest and Freddy by Gilles Tibo
Gabby's School by the Sea by Marie-Danielle Croteau
Grampy's Bad Day by Dominique Demers
John's Day by Marie-Francine Hébert
Peppy, Patch, and the Postman by Marisol Sarrazin
Peppy, Patch, and the Socks by Marisol Sarrazin
The Princess and the Frog by Margaret Nash
Rachel's Adventure Ring by Sylvia Roberge Blanchet
Run! by Sue Ferraby
Sausages! by Anne Adeney
Stickers, Shells, and Snow Globes by Dana Meachen Rau
Theodore the Millipede by Carole Tremblay
The Truth About Hansel and Gretel by Karina Law
When Nobody's Looking... by Louise Tondreau-Levert

Looking for a specific title or level? A complete list of *Read-it!* Readers is available on our Web site: *www.picturewindowbooks.com*